For Rob

For my

STRIPES PUBLISHING
An imprint of the Little Tiger Group
1 The Coda Centre, 189 Munster Road,
London SW6 6AW

A paperback original
First published in Great Britain in 2017

Text copyright © Adam Frost, 2017
Illustrations copyright © Emily Fox, 2017
Back cover images courtesy of www.shutterstock.com

ISBN: 978-1-84715-774-4

Fox Investigates

A Dash of Poison

ADAM FROST
ILLUSTRATED BY EMILY FOX

Stripes

THE MUMMY'S CURSE

Wily Fox, the world's greatest detective, was inside the British Museum in London, looking at a display of Egyptian mummies. There were cats, dogs, monkeys and falcons – all wrapped up tightly in bandages.

Usually the room was full of visitors, but right now it was empty. It was 8 a.m. and the building was not yet open but Wily was there to meet the famous Egyptologist, Basil Buffalo.

As he peered at the mummies, Wily heard a voice behind him.

"I wouldn't get too close if I were you."

Wily turned to see a cleaning lady – a cheerful-looking raccoon wearing a scarf around her head and holding a large feather duster.

"Why not?" Wily asked.

"They're cursed," said the raccoon.

"Right," said Wily with a smile.

He moved across to the next cabinet and looked inside.

"Those are cursed, too," said the raccoon.

"OK," said Wily, moving along to another exhibit.

"Cursed," said the raccoon.

"OK..." said Wily. "Are any of the exhibits NOT cursed?"

"Hmm," said the raccoon. "This lot is safe." She pointed to a cabinet behind her. "But stay at this end. There's an amulet down there that is HIGHLY dubious."

"What makes you think everything here is cursed?" Wily asked.

"The animals that discovered them all died in *very* suspicious circumstances."

"Really," said Wily, raising an eyebrow.

The raccoon started cleaning another cabinet.

"I can't help noticing," Wily remarked, "that *you* don't seem to be worried about the curse. You're cleaning all the cabinets."

"Ah, yes," said the raccoon, "but that's because of these." She pointed to a tangle of necklaces and charms around her neck. "They protect against evil spirits," she said. "Tell you what, take this and then you can look at whatever you like."

She took off one of the necklaces and offered it to Wily but he held his hand up. "It's OK. You keep it."

Wily didn't believe in curses. Whenever animals died in suspicious circumstances, there was always a reason. The mystery might be wound up tight like a bandaged mummy but if you kept tugging, you could always unravel it.

Ten minutes later a security guard showed Wily into Basil Buffalo's office. It was full of Egyptian vases and statues. A tubby buffalo stood up and shook Wily's hand excitedly. His wool was grey and dusty and he had three pairs of glasses balanced on his head.

"Thank you so much for agreeing to see me," Basil Buffalo said. "Do sit down."

"It sounded urgent," Wily said, taking a seat.

Basil nodded. "It is. I need you to find a knife."

"A knife?" Wily replied. "Did you look in your cutlery drawer?"

"Well, it's more a dagger than a knife," Basil said with a smile, typing something into a computer on his desk. A projector beamed an image on to the wall. It showed a fragment of stone covered in hieroglyphics.

"Do you know what these mean, Mr Fox?" Basil asked, flipping one of his pairs of glasses down on to his nose.

Wily squinted at them. "I recognize some of the symbols but you can hardly see them."

"Exactly," Basil said. "This has been part of our collection for two hundred years. But because most of the hieroglyphics are worn away, nobody's been able to make head nor tail of the inscription. Every few years we throw a young researcher at it, to see if they can crack the code. And guess what? Last month, a very smart young vole worked it out! She used some clever computer program that I don't pretend to understand. Now we know what the hieroglpyhics say." He tapped the keyboard and the image changed.

> Find the lion's body and go on ahead.
> My weapon sleeps in the desert's bed.
> Silently, with a million cuts.
> From inside out, it shreds your guts.
>
> Menes

"Find the lion's body?" Wily wondered aloud. "Isn't there a huge statue in Egypt with a lion's body?"

"There is!" Basil said. "Near the pyramids of Giza. It's called the Sphinx."

"And you think there's a dagger hidden there?" Wily said.

"Yes, there's a trench north of the Sphinx that's never been excavated. I'm *sure* it's there."

"OK – so who's Menes?" Wily asked.

"He was one of the first pharaohs," said Basil, "and a great military commander. He won battles against impossible odds. In all the depictions of him he's holding a dagger but we didn't know it was real – until now."

"So you think the riddle reveals the location of the dagger?"

"I think so," replied Basil. "The riddle says: 'Silently, with a million cuts'. Doesn't that sound like a dagger to you?"

"Maybe," said Wily, rubbing his chin. "But why aren't you in Egypt digging it up?"

Basil stuck out his leg, revealing a foot in plaster. "I'm stranded. You see, the news of the hieroglyphics being decoded was top secret but two days ago, I made rather a large boo-boo. I told my mother about it. I was just so excited, you see. I swore her to secrecy but she couldn't help boasting to one of her oldest friends, Diana Donkey."

"Why's that a problem?"

"Because this is her son." Basil tapped at his computer again and a picture of a donkey appeared on the screen. "Doug Donkey," he explained. "We've been rivals ever since we were at school together but we've taken very different paths.

I give everything I find to museums and galleries but Doug sells what he finds to the highest bidder."

"You mean he's an antiques dealer?"

"I'm afraid he's worse than that. If he has to break the law to find relics, he will. He cheats and steals, then sells his treasure to rich criminals." Basil sighed. "Douglas has become something of a monster."

"I used to have a friend like that," Wily said. Klara Kraftypants had been top of the class when they were at detective school together but a year ago she'd built a mega-torpedo from plans she'd disguised as paintings. Wily had stopped her destroying the world with only seconds to spare.

"Old friends always make the worst enemies," Wily added. "What makes you think Doug's mum told him?"

"That's what our mothers do. My mother is always telling me how Doug has bought a yacht or a private jet. I keep explaining he's a criminal but she says I'm just jealous. And there's THIS, too." He pointed at his injured foot.

"Yesterday *someone* pushed me over, knocked me out and took my briefcase. It had my notes on the riddle inside."

"You saw it was Doug?"

"No, but it's his style, all right. And who else would do it?"

"Do you still have your coat or anything that the criminal might have touched?"

"Yes," said Basil, taking a large brown coat off a peg.

Wily put the coat to his nose. "There's a whiff of donkey on there. But my assistant Albert will check it over properly."

Basil nodded.

"One final question," Wily said. "Why didn't you tell the police?"

"Doug's too clever for the *police*," Basil said. "He's spent his whole life breaking the law and getting away with it." He grabbed one of Wily's paws. "Do say you'll take the case, Mr Fox. I know you can find the dagger for me and stop it falling into Doug's hands. It belongs HERE in a museum. Not in some billionaire's private collection."

Wily pulled his paw free and said, "I'll do it."

"Wonderful news!" Basil clapped his hands and jiggled up and down, sending all three pairs of glasses clattering to his desk. Then he handed Wily a piece of paper. "Here's a map of Giza. I've put a cross where I think the dagger is most likely to be."

"OK," Wily said, putting the map in his pocket. "I'd better go and stop Doug digging."

ALBERT CUTS A RUG

Wily returned to his office and immediately slid down the secret fireman's pole to Albert Mole's underground laboratory. Wily had already phoned Albert and given him a quick rundown on the case but now they needed to talk tactics.

"So this is the riddle," said Wily.

He passed Albert the piece of paper with the riddle written on it.

"Wow," said Albert. "I was aware of the ancient stone but I didn't realize it had been deciphered."

"So I'm off to Egypt to find this weapon before it falls into the wrong hands," continued Wily. "Basil thinks it's a dagger."

"Ah yes," said Albert. "Menes's famous dagger. You don't look convinced, though."

"Well, I didn't want to hurt the old guy's feelings," said Wily, "but it's a bit obvious, isn't it? 'A million cuts'. 'Shreds your guts'. It could be a dagger but aren't riddles supposed to be harder than that?"

"What do you think it is then?" Albert asked.

"I'm not sure yet," said Wily, "but the 'inside out' part is bugging me."

"Be careful, Wily – most of those Egyptian

treasures are protected by very powerful curses."

"Curses!" exclaimed Wily. "I had all that nonsense from the museum cleaner!"

"Dozens of Victiorian explorers visited the pyramids," said Albert, "and nearly all of them died soon after. Perhaps there's something alive down there." He shuddered.

"There's nothing living in the pyramids except dung beetles," said Wily, "but I need your help to find out who stole the briefcase from Basil. He thinks it was Doug Donkey." Wily gave Albert the buffalo's coat. "See what you can find on there," he said. "I detected donkey but there's something else, too."

"Will do," Albert said.

"And find out everything you can about Doug," Wily added. "I'd better get going. The criminal's got a day's head start on me."

"Well, I've got a new gadget that might speed things up," Albert said, hopping off his stool and heading to the other side of the laboratory. He pointed to a large patterned rug. "What do you think?" he asked, smiling proudly.

"Very nice," grunted Wily. "Matches the wallpaper. Now, where's the gadget?"

Albert put his fingers in his mouth and whistled. The rug lifted off the ground and hovered in front of the mole's nose.

"It's made of tensile metals so it's both strong and flexible," said Albert. "And it has a maximum speed of 593 miles per hour."

"A flying carpet!" Wily exclaimed.

"Basically," said Albert. "It can carry up to two animals at a time. I've programmed it to recognize your whistle as well as mine. You can speak your destination into this sensor at the top or steer it manually using the tassels at the corners. Clap twice to fold it up."

Wily jumped on. The carpet sank slightly then floated up again, wobbling gently as it adjusted to Wily's weight.

"Flying to the Nile in style," he murmured.

"Take this, too," said Albert, handing Wily a small black box. "It's an explorer's survival kit."

Wily flipped open the lid and saw some bandages, an advanced guide to hieroglyphics and a small vial of green liquid.

"This is an antidote," said Albert, pointing at the vial. "It counteracts every known kind of snake venom. But try not to get into any fights with snakes."

"I won't bother them if they don't bother me," said Wily. "I'll call you from Egypt."

He said, 'Giza, Egypt,' into the carpet's sensor and held on tight as it whizzed across the laboratory towards the long fireman's pole that led to his office and blasted up the shaft.

Wily clung on and whooped with excitement as the carpet zipped across his office, out of the window and up into the blue sky above.

Within thirty minutes, he was cruising over Paris. His phone pinged a few times. It was Albert.

> The fur on Basil's coat comes from a 56-year-old male donkey. Matches Doug's profile exactly. Also paw prints from an unknown animal. Possibly sloth or panda, hard to narrow it down further.

He opened the next mail.

> Doug Donkey is highly dangerous. Connected to the looting of the Lost City of Ware-Izzit, where three llama tour guides were found dead. Has links to criminal gangs across the world, particularly in Russia.

"Sounds like a deadly donkey," Wily said.

Finally Wily saw the pyramids and then the Sphinx, covered by scaffolding.

There were tourists milling around so Wily flew a bit further, away from the crowds, before touching down behind a large boulder. He clapped twice and the carpet folded itself up and leaped into his pocket.

He pulled out the map. Basil had made a cross to mark a trench next to a large sand dune north of the Sphinx. Wily started to walk towards it, past a row of stalls selling tourist postcards and T-shirts, and four snake-charmers making four cobras sway to the music.

When Wily reached the sand dune, he stopped. A set of donkey's hoofprints were clearly visible.

"Good of you to leave me a trail," he said.

He followed the prints up the side of the dune. Part of the way up, he spotted two more sets of prints, as well as some strange criss-crossing lines. They were all churned up together – it was impossible to identify who or what had made the new prints.

Had Doug beaten him to it and found the dagger?

As Wily was examining the prints, he spotted a strip of cloth poking out of the sand. He teased it out and saw that it had a number stitched into it:

0778-92-222

A phone number? Funny way to record it, Wily thought, putting the cloth in his pocket.

He reached the top of the dune and looked down the other side. There was a strange-shaped rock at the bottom of the dune – exactly where Basil had marked his X.

Wily headed towards it and realized that it wasn't a rock, it was a head.

As he ran closer, it became clear that the head belonged to a donkey.

"Get me out of here," the donkey gasped, opening his eyes slightly.

"What happened, mate?" Wily asked, putting on his thickest Australian accent. He was sure this donkey must be Doug but he didn't want to reveal his own identity.

"They buried me up to my neck in sand and left me here."

"Wow, you're lucky I came by," Wily said. "Shall I call the police?"

"No police," Doug said. "Just get me out. My trowel's by that rock over there."

Wily started to dig. "Any idea who did it?"

Doug shook his head. "They … wore masks."

"Blimey! That sounds frightening," Wily said. He stopped digging, "Hey, how do I know *you're* not some kind of criminal."

Doug sighed. "I'm an archaeologist. I was looking for something valuable. I dug a hole here but there was nothing. Then I looked up and these two ... bad guys ... started to fill the hole – with me still in it."

"But why?"

"They wanted to slow me down. I think they're after the same thing as I am."

"Wow, it must be pretty awesome, mate," said Wily, as he freed Doug's arms.

"It could be the most valuable artefact in the world," Doug said.

"But it's not where you thought it was?"

"No, but I know where to try next."

Wily was about to ask where, when he felt a sharp pain on his ankle. He looked down and saw the four cobras that had been swaying in front of the snake charmers. One had just bitten him.

"You're tressspasssing," it said.

Wily felt suddenly light-headed as the cobra's venom entered his bloodstream. He hit the cobra on the head with the trowel, knocking him out but the other three sped towards him, their fangs bared. Wily clapped twice and the flying carpet flew out of his pocket. He clambered on.

"Hey!" cried Doug. "What about me?"

Wily hesitated. Could he leave Doug there?

He held out the loose body of the cobra to Doug. "Hang on."

Doug grabbed the other end of the snake.

"Hold tight," Wily said, moving the carpet forwards and yanking Doug out of the hole.

The three cobras flung themselves at Doug.

"Missed – you slimeballs," Doug snarled,
grabbing the edge of the flying carpet and
climbing on. Wily dropped the snake and,
within a couple of seconds, they were zooming
over the Great Pyramid.

"Sorry to have to do this," Doug said.

"Do what?" Wily said.

"You're clearly not an Australian tourist,"
Doug said. "Not with a gadget like this.
Fortunately I always carry a spare trowel."

Doug hit Wily as hard as he could with the
trowel and shoved him off the carpet.

THE GREAT PYRAMID

Wily opened his eyes and stared up at the sky. How long had he been out for? The sun was high in the sky – midday had come and gone.

His head was pounding and the snakebite seemed to have paralyzed his legs. He took the explorer's kit from his coat pocket and took a swig of the antidote Albert had given him. The effect was immediate – he gasped with relief and sat up.

Looking around, he realized that he'd landed on the top of the Great Pyramid of Giza. No

animals were allowed to climb the pyramid,
so if the snakes were looking for him, they
wouldn't find him up here.

He tried whistling for his flying carpet but it
didn't appear.

Next he called Albert and gave him a quick
rundown of what had happened.

"So Doug's a rotter all right," Albert said.

"Yes, but it sounds like the animals who buried him are even more ruthless," said Wily. "I need to work out who they are and how they got hold of the riddle."

"Any ideas?" Albert asked.

"I found a clue – a number written on a strip of cloth. Right near where I found Doug."

Wily held up the strip to the screen.

"Could be a phone number with a couple of digits missing," Albert said.

"That's what I thought," Wily said. "Can one of your clever computers work out the missing numbers?"

"Probably," Albert said. "I'll run it through some decryption software. Leave it with me."

"Thanks," said Wily. "And can you tell me anything else about this dagger? I know it's valuable but why are so many animals this determined to get it?"

"OK," said Albert, "I'll put together a dossier on Menes. You'll see why the dagger is so famous."

"One last thing," Wily said. "You know the flying carpet…"

"Wily! What have you DONE?" Albert wailed.

"Nothing…" said Wily. "But say I *did* lose it and I *whistled* for it, shouldn't it come back?"

Albert frowned. "Yes. It's got a range of thousands of miles. Unless it's somewhere completely soundproof, of course."

"OK, thanks," Wily said. "Gotta go." He ended the call before Albert had a chance to protest.

Next he called Basil. Wily saw the side of Basil's chin and heard him muttering, "Is this working?" before the buffalo finally appeared on screen and declared, "This is my first video call. How exciting!"

"I need to keep it brief," Wily said. "The dagger wasn't where you thought. I'm going to have to look further afield."

"Really?" Basil looked crestfallen, "I-I felt sure it would be there."

"You're not the only one," said Wily. "Doug got the place wrong, too. And so did someone else."

"Someone else?"

"Yes," Wily added. "I'm afraid there are other animals on the trail of the dagger and I think they have hired a team of snakes to help them."

"Snakes?" Basil said.

"Any idea who that might be?" Wily asked.

"No," Basil said, shaking his head.

"Or where they might look for the dagger next?"

Basil shook his head again. "This is awful, Mr Fox. I'm no help at all."

"Don't worry. I'll dig out the answers and update you soon," Wily said, ending the call.

Where was the dagger? he wondered.

"'Find the lion's body and go on ahead'," Wily muttered, repeating the first line of the riddle. "Ahead. A head."

What if it wasn't "go on ahead" but "go on a head"? Go on to the head of the Sphinx!

He pulled out his phone and opened the Binoculars app to look more closely at the Sphinx. The scaffolding around it meant that its head was obscured but he could see a trail of donkey's hoofprints in the sand between its paws. Had Doug landed the carpet in front of the Sphinx?

Wily clambered down the pyramid as fast he could and ran towards the giant statue. It was early evening now and there were hardly any tourists about.

He looked around to see if there were any guides or guards but they seemed to have gone home, too, so he ducked behind the scaffolding.

He climbed up one of the scaffolding poles and leaped on to a plank that sat across the Sphinx's back.

There was a narrow board leading from there to the Sphinx's neck and head and Wily could see more faint tracks on this plank. Not just a donkey's this time but also a snake's – and was that a fox's paw print? Surely not.

He wondered whether he was had hit his head when he landed on top of the pyramid. Was he seeing things?

There were two wavy lines, too – like someone had tried to rub the tracks out.

"I reckon I'm in the right place," Wily muttered. "But where is everyone?"

He looked around. He could feel something. A change in temperature. A breeze. Where was it coming from? He held his hand out and felt his palm growing colder. Air was rising up from somewhere.

He got down on his knees so he could reach the Sphinx's head. There was a square of stone that was loose.

Was Doug INSIDE the Sphinx?

He tried lifting up the loose stone but it wouldn't budge so he tried pushing it down instead. The Sphinx's neck turned into a flight of steps leading into a hole in its back.

"'My weapon sleeps in the desert's bed'," Wily said, reciting the second line of the riddle. "Looks like we're going underground."

"Oh no, you're not," said a voice.

Two animals stepped out from behind a flap of tarpaulin.

"Julius!" Wily said. "What on earth is PSSST doing in Egypt?"

Detective Julius Hound and Sergeant Sybil Squirrel worked for PSSST – the Police Spy, Sleuth and Snoop Network.

"I'm asking the questions, Fox," Julius said, "and you can start by answering this one. Why shouldn't I arrest you for criminal damage to a world-famous monument?"

"Give him a break, Sarge," Sybil said. "We've spent the last half hour trying to work out how to get inside."

"I-I knew exactly how to activate those steps," Julius huffed. "I just wanted to … give you a chance to work it out, Sybil."

"For the last ten minutes you've had your head stuck up the Sphinx's left nostril," said Sybil, "but Wily's found a way inside in a couple of minutes. It's hardly fair to arrest him."

"Grrrr. OK. But tell us exactly what you're doing here," Julius said, putting his face right up against Wily's.

Wily smiled. "Holiday."

Julius snorted and Sybil burst out laughing.

"You've never taken a holiday in your life, Wily," she said.

"I know, but I wanted to see what all the

fuss was about," Wily said, "and I can see why they're popular. You meet so many interesting new animals…"

"You're on a case," barked Julius, "and let me tell you – it better not be the same as OUR case or you'll be in big trouble."

"Tell me what your case is then," Wily said.

"Absolutely not," said Julius. "It's one hundred per cent classified."

"It wouldn't be connected to a donkey, would it?" Wily asked.

Julius looked baffled and shook his head. "What donkey?"

"Or a priceless dagger?" Wily asked.

Julius shook his head again.

Wily looked at Sybil and she also shrugged and said, "No daggers."

"Hmm," Wily said. "But your crook is in the Sphinx."

"We're not sure," Sybil said. "This is their last known location. Made a mobile call first thing this morning and then—"

"Enough, Sybil," Julius growled. "He knows too much already. Listen, Fox. You stay right here." He turned to face Sybil. "Sybil, you and I need to complete our investigation. Keep behind me at all times and make sure Wily Fox doesn't follow us or—"

"He's gone, Sarge," Sybil said.

"What?" said Julius, turning round.

"He's gone," Sybil repeated.

Julius watched as Wily hurried down the steps and disappeared into the darkness.

"Blast that fox!" Julius snarled, stomping after Wily.

THE SHIVERING SANDS

Wily, Julius and Sybil walked all the way down the steps until they finally emerged into a huge underground chamber. Light streamed in from the opening where they'd entered the Sphinx. They saw animal tracks on the floor, criss-crossing a carpet of fine sand. Small black scarab beetles scuttled to and fro. On one of the walls, there was a large painting of an Egyptian pharaoh. On the other side of the vault, there was a small door.

Wily moved across to take a closer look at

the painting. The pharaoh – a noble-looking camel – was holding something in his hand. On either side of him, two wolves were holding their stomachs.

Sybil came over to take a look. "Who's the camel?"

"Menes," said Wily, pointing at a row of hieroglyphics in the corner of the painting.

"Who's Menes?" Sybil asked.

"An Egyptian pharaoh," said Wily, "I'm looking for something that belonged to him."

"The dagger you mentioned earlier?" Sybil asked.

Wily nodded. "He might have hidden it here."

Sybil smiled. "I didn't think you were on holiday." She squinted up at the picture. "So that's the dagger he's holding?"

Wily was looking closely. "Probably. It's just weird that..."

"What?"

"Would you hold a dagger by the blade like that?"

"Oh yeah," Sybil said.

In the painting, Menes was holding the blade of the dagger and pointing the handle up at the sky.

46

"Wouldn't that hurt?" Wily muttered.

"I guess so," Sybil said. "If it was sharp enough to kill those guys." She pointed at the wolves that were depicted next to the pharaoh, holding their stomachs.

Wily took a picture of the painting and sent it to Albert. At the same time, he heard a loud bark behind him.

Sybil and Wily span round and saw Julius up to his waist in sand.

"I'm sinking," Julius growled. "Get me out of here!"

"Hang on, boss! I'm coming!" Sybil said.

She moved carefully, trying to work out where the normal sand stopped and the quicksand started.

"In your own time!" Julius barked, who was now up to his neck.

Sybil's foot started to sink and she yanked it out. "This is impossible!" she cried. "It'll suck us in, too."

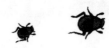

"It's a trap," Wily said.

Julius's growl was cut off as his head sank under the sand.

"He's going to die!" Sybil exclaimed.

"OK," Wily said. "Hold on to my hands and lower me in."

Sybil held Wily's hands tightly and lowered him into the sand.

"If I tug twice, pull me out," Wily said.

"Wily, w-wait…" Sybil stammered.

But it was too late. Wily was completely swallowed up – just his arms poked out. He reached for Julius with his feet. Nothing. He swivelled round, kicking out left and right.

He could feel himself starting to suffocate. He didn't have long but he needed to get further down to find Julius. He let go of one of Sybil's hands and reached slightly deeper.

Still no Julius.

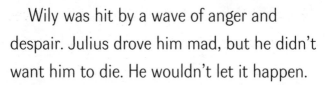

Wily was hit by a wave of anger and despair. Julius drove him mad, but he didn't want him to die. He wouldn't let it happen.

He stretched further, only a single finger still connecting him to Sybil.

At last he felt something. He hooked it with his toe and pulled. It barely moved in the thick sand, so he pulled harder and finally he managed to get both his feet round Julius's neck.

Now to get out. He tugged Sybil's hand. Could she feel it? He tugged again.

Sybil began hauling him – and an unconscious Julius – out of the sand.

"That was totally insane, Wily," Sybil said, checking Julius's pulse.

Wily wiped the sand out of his nose and ears. "Is he alive?"

Sybil nodded. "But he'll probably be zonked out for a while."

"Perfect," Wily said, standing up. "That gives us time to work this out."

"Work what out?"

"First, how we get across this room without dying," Wily said.

"Right."

"Second, what happened to Doug and the others? Did they get across?"

"Doug? Who's he?"

"Third," Wily continued, ignoring Sybil's question. "Why so much protection? I mean, if Menes did hide his dagger down here, why kill anyone who's looking for it?"

"I guess he loved his dagger," Sybil said.

"Maybe. Or maybe it's not just a dagger," said Wily. "It could be something more powerful. We *have* to find it first."

"We? Wily – I'm on a different case..."

Wily was moving around the edge of the

quicksand. "Help me with mine, then I'll help you with yours. Hey, look at this."

He pointed at a particularly confusing trail of animal tracks.

"Julius must have been looking at these before he wandered into the quicksand," Wily said. "Those are his paw prints there."

"And those are donkey's hooves," Sybil said. "You mentioned a donkey, right?"

Wily looked at the smudged trail next to Doug's. Instantly he remembered seeing the same marks on the scaffolding outside. At the same time, an image dropped into his head: snakes moving across a sand dune.

"I've got a theory," Wily said. "Two groups of crooks came through here. The first group contained three animals. Two mammals and a snake. The snake travels behind the mammals. Why? Because as he moves, he wipes out their tracks."

"Hmm. Clever," Sybil said.

"A few hours later, Doug Donkey arrives," said Wily. "As far as I know, he's working alone. The first group have already tried to slow Doug down by burying him alive. But he's escaped and he's determined to catch up."

"Looks like some of them made it across," Sybil said.

She pointed at the door on the other side of the room. There were faint tracks around the door frame. Wily pulled out his phone and opened the Binoculars app.

"It looks like they ALL made it," Wily said.

"I suspect Doug flew across on the flying carpet, but what about the first group?"

"Wait – flying carpet?"

"One of my gadgets fell into the wrong hands," Wily said. "But the first group would have had to use a different method."

Wily studied the sand again. Scarab beetles were still scuttling back and forth.

"There's no way round it – or over it," Sybil said, looking at the walls and ceiling.

Then Wily looked at the beetles again. "Hang on! Look at the scarabs."

"What about them?" Sybil said.

"They're not sinking," Wily said.

"They must know the way across," Sybil whispered.

Slowly and carefully, Wily trod on the sand, following the path of the beetles.

"Coming?" Wily said, looking behind him.

Sybil glanced at Julius, who was sleeping soundly in the corner.

"I should probably stay with the boss," she said.

"The fun's this way," Wily said, pointing ahead.

Sybil smiled and followed Wily across the sand.

"Time to explore," Wily said, as they reached the door on the other side.

SYBIL'S FOR THE CHOP

Wily and Sybil walked down a narrow tunnel into the next vault.

This one was smaller with a large statue of Menes in the centre and what looked like a large wishing well in front of it.

Wily headed for the statue and examined it. Menes was holding a large pot with a scorpion, a cobra and a spider painted on the side.

At the same moment, Wily heard his phone beep. Thanks to the booster chip that Albert had installed last month, the signal was still strong. He reached into his pocket and pulled it out. There was an email from Albert.

Wily skimmed through the information about Menes and his dagger, reading out the key passages to Sybil.

"'Menes's dagger was passed down from father to son until it went missing in the reign of Userkaf'. Maybe that's when they built this place..."

"Maybe," Sybil said. She had wandered over to the well.

"'If Menes was wearing his magic dagger, he could simply point his finger at an enemy and they would expire there and then'," Wily read. "But that's not possible..." he added. He looked again at the statue of Menes. "'Silently, with a million cuts. From inside out, it shreds your guts'," he repeated to himself.

Then he opened his eyes wide. "Sybil, I'm certain that this isn't a dagger."

"OK..." she said, peering down the well.

"Think about it. The painting. People grabbing their stomachs. Being killed *from inside out*. Menes holding the dagger by the blade – like it was a vial or a bottle."

"So what are you thinking?" she asked.

"I think it's POISON," Wily said. "Look at this statue. He's holding a cooking pot. What are the symbols on the side? Scorpions. Spiders. Cobras. All *venomous*. Maybe the venom from these animals is in the poison."

"I guess."

"Albert said Menes could just point at his enemy and they'd die. That's impossible. Unless Menes *knew* they were about to drop. Because, for example, he'd *poisoned* their dinner. And last of all, the thing that's been bugging me from the start. Why does everyone care so much about this dagger? Enough to risk their LIVES for it. If it's a deadly poison, it's not surprising that a bunch of dangerous criminals want to get their hands on it. It's a serious weapon."

"Oh no," Sybil said, seeming to remember something, "I think you might be right."

"I think I might be right, too. But who? Who are these criminals?"

Sybil fell silent and refused to meet Wily's eye.

At the same time, Wily texted Albert.

Any progress on the strip of cloth with the number on?

As he texted back, he heard Sybil say, "Wily, I think we have to jump down this well. It's the only other way out of this chamber."

"OK," Wily mumbled, rereading his message and pressing Send.

Then Sybil shrieked.

Wily raced to the well and saw Sybil dangling from the edge by her fingers. Below her, circular blades whirled back and forth and spears shot out from the walls of the well.

"I can't hold on!" Sybil yelled.

Wily tried to grab Sybil's arm as she lost her grip. She dropped – then managed to grab a ledge, just above the first whizzing blade.

"Wily, the stone is crumbling away," Sybil said, her terrified voice echoing around the well. "I'm going to be cut to pieces."

"Hang on!" Wily cried. "I'll think of something!"

He looked up at the room. The statue of Menes glowered down at him.

"OK," Wily said, "you have to trust me. When I say NOW, press yourself against the wall – as flat as you can."

"A-all right," Sybil gibbered. "But hurry."

Wily stood behind the statue and pushed it as hard as he could. It wobbled slightly.

"I'm slipping," Sybil said.

"Nearly there," Wily said, giving the statue another push. The grinding blades seemed to be getting louder.

"It's no good. Wily, I'm losing my grip."

The statue wasn't budging. It was time for one last attempt. He ran across to the edge of the room and frowned at the statue. He was ten metres away – that was a long enough run-up. He was ready to try one of his most secret and lethal kung-fu moves.

Sybil howled, "WILY!"

Wily shouted, "NOW!"

He did a triple backflip, followed by a mid-air somersault and then struck the head of the statue with the most powerful double-footed kick he had ever unleashed.

The statue juddered forwards and fell into the well.

It whistled past Sybil – missing her by millimetres – and crashed down into the shaft, smashing past the swords and spears and saws and blades.

The blades kept slicing as the statue fell, knocking off its edges and sides.

By the time the statue reached the bottom of the well, it had been smashed to pebbles and powder, but the blades had also ground to a halt.

"That was a close shave," Wily said. He called down to Sybil, "I'm coming to pick you up."

Wily took off his coat and used it like a parachute, leaping down the well and grabbing Sybil as he fell. They landed at the bottom with a gentle *whoomph*.

"Anything broken?" Wily said.

"Just the statue," Sybil said. "You realize that was a priceless artefact?"

"Yeah, well, so am I," said Wily. "Now, where are we?"

They looked around at another huge chamber. It seemed to have no entrance other than the shaft they'd come down. On the walls were more paintings of Menes. The floor was sandy again but this time there were tracks *everywhere.*

"What happened here?" Sybil murmured.

Wily spotted donkey tracks leading away from three strips of shredded metal. There were a few splats of blood on the sand around it.

"That was my flying carpet," Wily said, peering at the metal. "It looks like Doug used it to get past those blades in the well. He seems to have made it in one piece, but my carpet didn't."

Sybil was on her knees. "There are at least three sets of animal tracks here. How did *they* get down the well alive?"

Wily spotted a small stone button jutting out from the sand, directly below the hole. Did that control the weapons? He jumped on the button and the swords in the well groaned and clanked above them. He jumped on it again and they wheezed to a halt.

"Wow," said Wily. "Whoever got down through the well worked that out. They either targeted the button from the top of the well or they had someone in here do it for them."

Sybil nodded and looked at the tracks again.

"These criminals are seriously smart," Wily muttered. "I only know two animals capable of cracking a puzzle like that. Solomon Sneakychops and Klara Kraftypants. Solomon was an eccentric stoat who died in a freak hang-gliding accident three years ago. And Klara's where we put her a year ago – in prison."

"Mmm," said Sybil, avoiding Wily's gaze.

Wily bent down and looked at the tracks.

"There are donkey and snake tracks again, but there IS something else. Look, the snake hasn't rubbed everything out."

There was a large paw print close to one of the walls. Wily looked at its size and shape. The animal was two metres tall at least. He remembered Albert saying that the animal who had stolen Basil's briefcase was a panda, a sloth or a similar kind of animal. Was this the same creature? The paw print was bigger than a sloth's. It looked like a bear's…

At that moment, all the facts from one of his most famous cases tumbled back into his head. The Parisian Painting Plot. He remembered how the Russian bear, Dimitri Gottabottomitch, had helped his old schoolfriend Klara Kraftypants to assemble a mega-torpedo.

Was it Dimitri that had stolen Basil's briefcase? Was he here now?

Was Klara here, too?

She couldn't be. She was in a deep, dark cell in the Grisly Gorge Maximum Security Prison.

Or was she…?

He pulled out the strip of cloth from his pocket.

Q+78-92-222

Of course! It wasn't a phone number – it was a prisoner number, torn off a uniform.

He phoned Albert. "Albert, that phone number – it's not a phone number. I think it's a prisoner number. Can you find out Klara's prisoner number?"

"What?" Albert replied.

"Klara's prisoner number? What is it?"

Then Wily noticed Sybil on the other side of the room. She was staring directly at Wily with a guilty look on her face.

"It's OK, Albert, don't worry," Wily said. "I think I can find the answer here." Wily walked across to where Sybil was standing.

"I wanted to tell you," Sybil said. "You know I always tell you everything. But this time, I couldn't."

"Why?" Wily said, gritting his teeth.

68

"The boss has really messed up," Sybil said. "He would have killed me if I told you."

"Go on."

"Yesterday morning, Klara's prison put in an emergency transfer request," Sybil said. "She'd kidnapped the prison librarian – a highly strung hamster called Hubert – and dangled him out of the window by his ankles. They managed to stop her before she dropped him. But anyway, they decided to move her to Blackrock Island Prison where all the staff are robots. Julius thought she was up to something so he put himself in charge of transferring her. It was just me, him and Klara in the back of the security van. But the bear and his crew were waiting. They busted her out and beat us up. Now Julius wants to find Klara before anyone in PSSST realizes he's messed up."

"It's a bit late for that," Wily said.

"He thinks – if we find her – we can at least say that we foiled her break-out attempt and brought her back."

"Julius won't bring her back," Wily snarled. "She's way too clever for him."

"We'd managed to follow her trail this far," Sybil said. "But you're right. She would have blown up the world last time if you hadn't remembered how much she loved her favourite toy puffin."

"I beat her before," said Wily, "and I'll beat her again."

"And I'm going to help you," Sybil replied, with a determined look in her eye. "Whether you like it or not."

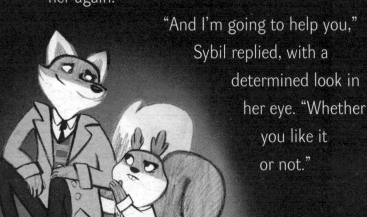

"OK. Then find out how they got out of this room. I have to pick Basil's brains."

Wily phoned Basil and gave him a speedy rundown of what had happened.

"So you think this Dimitri helped Doug to take my briefcase? But why?" Basil said.

"It's just a theory so far," Wily said. "But I think Doug told his usual contacts that he might have a precious dagger to sell them. He may even have mentioned Menes. Dimitri's an antiques dealer so he'd know exactly how much Menes's weapon was worth. He may have contacted Klara at that point or maybe he'd already decided to bust her out. I'm not sure."

"I see," said Basil. "But why would this Klara want the dagger?"

"Well, that's the other thing," Wily said. "Is there any way this dagger could be … something else? Like a powerful poison."

Basil said nothing.

"Basil, are you there?" Wily asked.

"Yes, yes, just thinking," Basil said.

"Well, speed up, I've got a fox to catch."

"You may be on to something," Basil said. "The hieroglyphic for spear or dagger is very similar to the hieroglyphic for poison. And then there are the pictures... I think we've always assumed Menes was holding a knife but – given the number of animals he killed and how they died – it could be..."

"What?"

"When the Egyptians buried their mummies, they always put powerful poisons around the lid of the sarcophogus. You've heard of all those Victorian explorers dying when they opened up a mummy's casket?"

"Yes."

"Well, we know now that it's because they

touched the poison on the lid. A poison so powerful that it was still deadly thousands of years later. Perhaps Menes INVENTED this deadly poison and stored it in a secret tomb."

"I bet Klara has worked this out already," Wily said.

"No, no," Basil said. "She can't have done. Impossible. She'd have to be the smartest animal that ever lived."

"Yep," Wily said. "That's her."

As Wily said the word "her", the air was split with an ear-splitting shriek.

"Got to go," Wily said. "This case really is a scream."

DOUG RISES
FROM THE DEAD

Wily and Sybil ran round the room, trying to work out where the scream was coming from.

There was a quieter shriek and then silence.

"Look!" Wily pointed at a square hole on the far wall that they hadn't noticed before.

Wily and Sybil scrambled up to it and discovered it was the entrance to another tunnel. As they shuffled along on their hands and knees, they heard a moan.

"It's a donkey braying," Wily said. "It must be Doug!"

They shuffled along faster and finally emerged in a giant circular chamber, ten times as big as any of the previous rooms.

Mummies lined the walls – there were hundreds of them. Some were in glittering caskets, others were open to reveal the bandaged animals. But there was no sign of any living creature.

"Maybe it wasn't Doug," Sybil said.

"Let's take a look around," Wily said. "But be careful. If Klara's here, anything could happen."

When Wily looked more closely at the mummies, he spotted that each had a strip of hieroglyphics under their feet. Taking out his book of hieroglyhpics, he decoded the letters.

We'll kill you with pleasure,
If you touch our precious treasure.
Only Menes and his successors,
Can be the drug's possessors.

"Looks like it was poison all right," said Sybil. "And these guys were put here to guard it. Not that they'd put up much of a fight."

"Maybe they would," Wily said, spotting something trickling down the edge of one of the caskets. "Basil said Egyptian coffins were always lined with poison."

He smelled the sticky liquid. His stomach immediately knotted and he felt incredibly sick. He stepped backwards as quickly as he could, gasping for air.

"Sybil, don't touch ANYTHING," he wheezed.

When his stomach had calmed down, Wily looked around the rest of the vault for traces of Klara or Doug – or the vial of poison.

One of the mummy's caskets had nothing inside. But there were hoofprints in front of it and that snake's swirling trail again.

That's odd, thought Wily.

At that moment, the moaning noise resumed and Sybil screamed. Wily span round and saw that the mummy directly behind Sybil was moving.

It tottered towards Sybil, arms outstretched. Sybil pulled out her truncheon and lifted it, ready to strike.

"No, Sybil! Stop!" Wily cried.

The mummy staggered for a few more steps, then collapsed.

Sybil lowered her truncheon and Wily pulled off the bandages from around the mummy's face.

It was Doug Donkey. "Thank you," he murmured.

"Whoa," Sybil said. "I could have killed him."

Doug half-smiled. "It's OK. Everyone's been trying to kill me today."

"Tell us what happened," Wily said.

"It's gone," Doug said. "They took it."

"What's gone?" Sybil asked.

"The vial," said Doug with a sigh.

"Who took it?" Wily asked.

"The bear," said Doug. "He tricked me again. He had a fox and a snake with him."

"Why didn't they just kill you?" Wily asked.

"It was the fox's idea to bandage me up," Doug said. "It seemed to amuse her. Said I'd die more slowly that way."

"OK. So what exactly happened in here?" Sybil asked.

"I'd followed them, but when I got here, the room was empty," Doug said wearily. "I started opening the caskets, looking for the dagger.

And I found it! Only it wasn't a dagger."

"Klara wanted *you* to open the caskets," said Wily. "She knew they were covered with poison."

"What?" Doug said.

"As soon as you picked up the vial," Wily said, "did she leap out and take it?"

"Pretty much," Doug said. "They'd been hiding the whole time. But hang on – you said I've been poisoned." He closed his eyes.

"You'll be OK," Wily said. "Try to think – did the fox mention anything about where she was going or why she wanted the poison?"

Doug shook his head.

Wily remembered the antidote Albert had given him. He took it out of his pocket and poured half of it down Doug's throat.

For a few seconds nothing happened. Then Doug sighed and smiled.

"Wow," he said. "I feel better already!"

"Sybil, are you OK to wait here and keep an eye on Doug until reinforcements arrive? I've got to find Klara. Fast."

Sybil nodded. "No problem, Wily."

"Doug, how did they get out of here?" Wily asked.

Doug nodded at a tiny gap high up in one of the walls. A yellow light glowed inside it.

"The snakes winched the fox and the bear up there," Doug said.

How am I going to reach that? Wily thought. Then he spotted a stone sticking out above the opening. He picked up a coil of bandage that lay in front of one of the mummy's caskets and flung it up towards the opening. On the third attempt he managed to loop the bandage over the stone. He tugged it and the bandage held.

He began to climb.

Halfway up, he looked down at Sybil. She was starting to unwrap Doug.

"I'd leave him tied up if I were you," Wily shouted. "He's not to be trusted."

Doug looked at Wily angrily but Sybil smiled and nodded. "Good idea."

Wily reached the opening and crawled inside the tunnel. He followed it until finally he emerged into daylight. His head was poking out of a hole in the Sphinx's bottom.

He looked down at the desert below. Klara, Dimitri and a snake were climbing into a dune buggy. Klara looked over her shoulder and saw Wily still stuck in the statue. She grinned and blew him a kiss.

Then Klara started up the buggy and they sped off.

DESERT RACERS

Wily looked around frantically for a way to get down from the Sphinx. As he did so, he saw another sand buggy charging along behind Klara.

Julius! He was still caked in sand and gunk but otherwise back to normal.

"Klara Kraftypants," Julius yelled. "You won't escape me this time!"

Wily peered down at the buggy Julius was driving. He would have to time his jump correctly if he was going to make it...

Just as Julius swerved around the back of the Sphinx, Wily leaped and landed with a jolt in the seat beside Julius.

"Thought I'd drop by," Wily said.

"The last thing I need is a hitchhiker," Julius snarled.

"Can't you go any faster?" Wily said. He filled Julius in about the poison that Klara had stolen.

"You should have waited for me!" Julius snapped. "No wonder you messed everything up."

"Me? This is YOUR mess. YOU let Klara escape from prison! And now she's escaping again. Come on – speed up!"

Julius accelerated towards Klara's buggy.

As they got closer, Dimitri climbed into the back of the buggy, picked up a vase and aimed it at Julius.

It missed its target and bounced away.

"Ha! Pathetic!" barked Julius.

Dimitri picked up a second vase. This time it hit Julius on the forehead, knocking him out instantly. The buggy veered off course and ground to a halt in the side of a dune.

"Sorry, Julius," Wily said, "but it's time to leave you behind again."

He dragged Julius out of the buggy, propped him up in the sand, then climbed into the driver's seat and put his foot down.

In less than a minute he had caught up with Klara's buggy.

Dimitri threw another vase but Wily swerved and it thudded into the sand.

Klara steered to the left and the buggy started to climb a huge sand dune. Dimitri hurled another vase at Wily but missed again. He bellowed in frustration and threw himself on to the bonnet of Wily's buggy. Wily swerved left and right, trying to throw the bear off, but Dimitri clung on. Then Dimitri heaved himself over the windscreen and put his giant paws around Wily's throat. The two animals wrestled furiously as the buggy raced along. Wily made a sudden swerve to the right and turned the buggy on to its side. At the same time, he pressed the button that popped open the boot.

Both Wily and Dimitri rolled down to the bottom of the dune, followed by the contents of the boot – a spare tyre, a car jack and a coil of rope.

Wily thought fast. He got to his feet, grabbed the tyre and yanked it down over Dimitri's head, pinning the bear's arms to his sides. Then, as the bear struggled, Wily tied his legs together tightly with the rope.

Dimitri glared at Wily and bared his teeth. "Let me go."

"Of course," said Wily. "If you answer my questions. Why did you break Klara out of prison?"

Dimitri shook his head and said nothing.

"OK," said Wily. "Enjoy the sunshine. I reckon you'll survive for a good two hours in this heat." He started to walk away, as Dimitri tried to get to his feet, fell over and then said, "OK, OK. I'm talking."

Wily strolled back.

"After Doug and I stole the briefcase," Dimitri said, "I took a photo of the riddle and told Klara about it."

"Why?"

"She's been waiting for the right moment to get her revenge and I knew that Menes is one of her heroes. Klara figured out instantly that the riddle wasn't about a dagger. An hour later, I got an encrypted video file from her.

She'd forced the prison librarian to record it. The message said that the riddle was about a poison that had the power to change the world. She told me she had a plan worked out and set up a meeting point."

"So how did the snakes get involved?"

"Untie me and I'll tell you," Dimitri said, struggling again.

Wily shook his head. "Not yet."

Dimitri snarled and then said, "Fine. That was Klara, too. She knew the snakes were familiar with the pyramids."

"Did she know the poison would be inside the Sphinx?"

"Of course," said Dimitri. "She said it was obvious from the riddle."

"So why did you go to the trench where Doug was digging?"

"She wanted him out of the way," said

Dimitri. "She knew he'd go to the wrong place. So we found him and we buried him."

"I know," said Wily. "I rescued him. So – final question. What's she going to do with the poison?"

"That I don't know," said Dimitri, shrugging.

"Come on, Dimitri," Wily said, "she must have told you something."

Dimitri shook his head and smiled. "She said information was on a need-to-know basis. And I didn't need to know."

Wily went through the bear's pockets and pulled out a map of America with numbers marked on it and a book containing tide times for the Atlantic and Pacific Oceans.

"So what are these for?"

Dimitri shrugged. "She gave them to me for safekeeping," he said, "but she didn't tell me what they were for."

"She told you nothing? About where you were going next?"

Wily held out the map of America.

"She said she wanted to put on a show on the world's biggest stage," replied Dimitri. "I thought she meant Russia, of course."

Wily put the map in his pocket. At the same moment, he saw Julius stomping angrily up the dune towards them.

"I think you have a visitor," said Wily. He rolled the dune buggy back on to its wheels and climbed in. "It looks like he's overheated," Wily added. "I'd better make tracks."

He roared off, covering Julius and Dimitri in a cloud of sand.

WILY THE STOWAWAY

Half an hour later, the dune buggy screeched to a halt next to a long airstrip.

Cairo airport.

Wily had to get to America – fast. Klara wanted to put on a show on the world's biggest stage and she'd given Dimitri a map of America's rivers. She must be planning to poison someone or something in America.

At one end of the runway, there was a large cargo plane, with polecats in blue overalls wheeling wooden crates up its loading ramp.

Wily opened the Flight Checker app on his spyphone and scanned the number on the plane's wing. The flight information appeared:

Destination: San Francisco, USA
Departure time: 7.30 p.m.

Perfect – it was leaving in five minutes.

A polecat trotted down the loading ramp and waved at the pilot, indicating that he should close the loading door.

"Time to check in," Wily said. He put his foot down on the accelerator and steered the dune buggy towards the ramp.

He crunched over a metal security fence and roared along the runway. As the rear door started to rise, Wily sped up. The buggy started to wobble and rattle but Wily still wasn't close enough. The pilot started the engine and the plane began to move. Suddenly Wily slammed on the brakes, flipping the buggy up and over in a huge somersault. It landed with a crunch on the loading ramp just before it closed. Then the buggy trundled down into the plane's cargo hold.

"We have lift-off," Wily said, sitting back.

Once the plane had started cruising, Wily made a video call to Albert to update him. "I've sent you an image of a map I took from Dimitri. It's covered in crosses and numbers. See what you make of it."

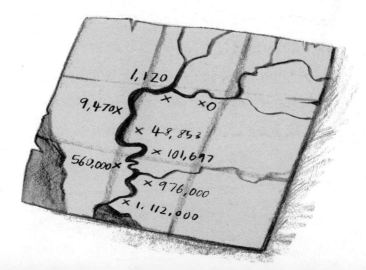

"I'm trying to work out where Klara might be headed," Wily added, looking at the map.

"Hmm," Albert said. "Those crosses are probably towns."

"I wondered about that," Wily said. "So what are the numbers? Altitude? Population?"

"No, they can't be," said Albert. "That cross there is probably Bitter Springs. It's about 1,500 metres up. Population is about 450. The cross has 48,853 next to it."

"Which of these towns is the biggest?" Wily asked. "Dimitri said Klara wanted a big stage."

"Lake Havasu City," said Albert, "but there's no airport and I'm afraid I haven't finished building a new flying carpet yet."

"That's fine," said Wily, "but you can send me something else. That snake antidote you gave me saved Doug Donkey's life."

"Oh good," said Albert. "It was a

concentrated formula designed to neutralize all poisons. My own recipe."

"Send me more," said Wily. "Lots more."

"I'll get cooking," said Albert.

Wily hung up and looked again at the map. He needed to get to Lake Havasu City. There was only one problem: the plane was headed for San Francisco – which was miles away! He could hardly ask the pilot to drop him off.

There was a tiny window in the side door of the cargo hold. Wily peered out and saw nothing but blackness – they must be flying over the sea, so he didn't need to figure out his exit strategy yet.

His phone buzzed. Basil.

"You're still alive! Thank goodness!" Basil said. "Was it poison?"

"Yes," said Wily, "and Klara's got it. But don't worry, I'll get it back. You'll still have an amazing artefact for your museum."

"Oh, don't worry about that any more," Basil said. "Listen, I have important information. I just got a call from one of my friends at the Smithsonian Museum in Washington."

"What did they say?" Wily asked.

"That two hours ago someone broke into their map department," said Basil. "Very strange."

"Why was it strange?"

"The thief only took old maps of Arizona. Ones showing weather patterns, waterways, where dams were built and so forth."

Wily's mind raced, connecting this new information to the map and the book Dimitri had been keeping for Klara. "Interesting," he said.

"There's more," added Basil. "The intruder was a snake."

"A snake? You're sure?"

"Positive," said Basil. "He was caught on their cameras. Their first break-in for fifty years and it's on the same day that your friend takes our poison."

Wily thanked Basil and hung up. It could be a coincidence but it didn't feel like it.

What was Klara doing? What was the link between an Egyptian poison and the weather in America?

He thought back to his time in detective school with Klara. What had they been taught? If you're being followed, throw them off the scent – fast. Put down lots of false trails. Send them off in the wrong direction. Is that what was happening here? Was Klara *not* going to America after all?

Before he knew it, they were flying over land and the sun was rising. He used the

GPS function on his phone to figure out their location. It was time to get off the plane. Now. But how? Could anything in the plane help?

He glanced around him at the rows and rows of crates. He lifted up one of the lids – packets of tea and coffee. No use.

Then he saw a giant crate covered in a tarpaulin. This gave him an idea. An insane idea.

He pulled off the tarpaulin and started to fold it up. Then he tied the corners down to the edges of the dune buggy's boot and stuffed it in. Next he looked for the button that controlled the loading door and pressed it. As the door opened, the wind thumped in his ears and the cold air made his eyes water.

Arizona.

He climbed into the dune buggy, started the engine and put his foot down.

The buggy sailed out into the air.

Wily looked down. Rocks and boulders dotted the landscape. Here and there, rivers were winding in and out of small towns. To the west, he could see the Colorado River.

The dune buggy plummeted down to the desert below. When it was around one hundred metres above ground level, Wily popped open the boot. The giant tarpaulin flapped open, forming a huge parachute. Nothing happened for a few seconds and then the buggy jerked upwards and began to descend slowly to the ground.

Wily breathed a sigh of relief.

A few seconds later the buggy landed in the sand. Wily leaned over and untied the tarpaulin – he was ready to go.

"Plane sailing," Wily said, zooming off.

THIRSTY WORK

As Wily sped through the desert towards Lake Havasu City, a text arrived from Albert:

Have mixed up more antidote. Will dispatch by drone.

"Thanks, Albert," Wily said to himself. "Now I just have to find Klara and get that poison."

Wily passed a row of cactuses, followed by a large rock and then another row of cactuses. Nothing else seemed to grow. His tongue started to feel dry as the temperature rose further. He was desperate for water.

Then everything clicked. WATER.

He pulled over and yanked the map out of his pocket. The Colorado River. All these crosses were towns on the Colorado River.

The snake was stealing maps of rivers and dams and rainfall and Dimitri had a book of tide times.

Klara must be planning to poison the water. It was the sort of thing she'd do – cruel and crazy.

Wily ran the theory through his head. If Klara poisoned the Colorado River it would flow into the sea. From there, poison would get into the rain, the ground, food, drink, baths, showers – everything.

Millions would die.

He had to stop her.

Once Fox had reached the centre of Lake Havasu City, he parked his buggy next to the Colorado River and leaped out. Crouching down, he put his nose to the water and breathed in, seeing if he could detect any of the smell he had inhaled inside the Sphinx.

Nothing. He wasn't too late.

There was only one problem. The Colorado River was over 2,000 kilometres long and his idea that Klara would be at Lake Havasu City was just a guess. If he was wrong, he'd have a lot of river to check.

He glanced up and down the water, looking for anything suspicious. Nothing seemed odd – there were animals fishing, sailing or strolling along the shore.

He clipped on his phone's headset and

called Albert. "Can you hack into one of PSSST's satellites? Look for anything suspicious or unusual along the river."

"Sure," said Albert. "Doing it now."

Then Wily phoned Sybil.

"Wily – where are you?" she said.

"Arizona," Wily said. "I'm going to need help. You and Julius must get here as soon as you can. And bring a ton of PSSST agents with you. I think Klara is planning to release the poison into the Colorado River."

"Wily," Sybil hissed, "Julius wants to string you up. I'll never talk him into this."

"Course you will. Got to go," Wily said, suddenly spotting something hovering above a bridge in the distance. As he ran towards it, he phoned Albert.

"There's a bridge at the end of the lake," Wily said. "I can see something above it."

"Got it on the satellite," said
Albert. "It's a chopper."

Wily kept running and
activated his Binoculars app.

Zooming in, he saw what looked like
a snake being lowered on to the bridge.
Something was in its mouth – could that
be the poison? Wily spoke to Albert on his
headset: "I think it's one of Klara's snakes."

"The helicopter's moving off," Albert said.

"Keep tracking it on the satellite," Wily said.
"I'll stop the snake."

The snake seemed to have stopped in the
middle of the bridge, resting his chin on the
edge.

*He's waiting for Klara to give him the go
ahead*, Wily thought to himself.

Wily sprinted along the bank and scrambled up to the bridge. The snake still seemed to be holding the bottle, waiting. There were cars and buses zipping along on both sides.

Wily had to be careful. One false move and the snake would pour the poison into the water.

At that moment, a couple of elderly warthogs began waddling across the bridge. Perfect. Wily slipped behind them, keeping step.

Wily could see that the snake was still waiting, grasping the bottle.

The warthogs seemed to slow down.

"No," whispered Wily to himself. "Keep walking, keep walking."

They stopped and looked over the edge of the bridge. At the same time, the snake seemed to tilt forwards.

Wily sprang out from behind the warthogs and sprinted as fast as he could towards the snake.

When the snake saw Wily, he dropped the bottle. "Pleassssse," he hissed. "Don't hurt me!"

Wily slammed into the snake and they both tumbled to the ground.

"It's just an empty bottle," stammered the snake. "She made me do it! She said she'd poison my family!"

Wily scrambled to his feet and looked down at the snake. He was young and his eyes were wide with terror. He wasn't one of Klara's gang.

"It's OK," Wily said. "I believe you."

Wily picked up the bottle. It had a piece of paper wrapped around it with an elastic band.

BOTTOM OF THE CLASS
AGAIN, WILY?
KLARA XXX

THE GRAND FINALE

How had he been so stupid?

In their very first detective class, they'd been taught how to buy time by setting up a decoy. It only has to look half real – your victim will do the rest.

He'd wanted to believe that the snake was one of Klara's sidekicks so he hadn't looked properly. He should have noticed the jerky movements that suggested someone acting against their will. Klara had been one step ahead of him the whole time.

Albert came through on his headset. "Did you stop the snake, Wily?"

"Yes," said Wily flatly.

"OK," said Albert. "Well, there are more. The helicopter is dropping animals – snakes, weasels, wolves – on every bridge along the river."

"Right," said Wily.

"She's not taking any chances, is she?" Albert continued. "The antidote won't get to you for at least half an hour. You have to stop those other animals."

Time was short but Wily wouldn't rush. He would think about his enemy this time.

He told Albert that the snake had been a decoy. "And I think some of those other animals might be decoys. Maybe all of them. She's relying on me making another basic mistake."

He looked down at the note Klara had written. He remembered their class on analyzing notes and letters at detective school.

"They can't all be decoys," Albert said. "She must be releasing the poison into the water somewhere."

Wily looked at the note again.

It wasn't just him who was in a hurry. Klara was, too. Plus she was feeling confident. She could make a basic mistake – he just had to slow down and LOOK.

"Wily, can you hear me?" Albert said.

Then he saw it. On the note, there was a faint indentation. He pulled out his pencil and started to shade. Slowly the words appeared. Klara had left a mark of what she had written on the page before.

TELL THE SNAKES TO MEET ME AT THE GRAND CANYON.

The Grand Canyon. Wily pulled out the map again. That was it. Marked with a zero.

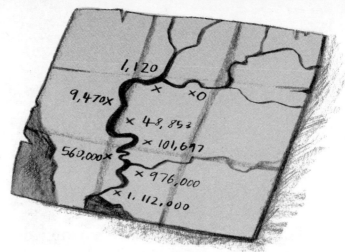

That was the world's biggest stage.

And now the writing on the map made sense, too. They were adding up the numbers of animals in each city the river flowed past. The number of animals who would DIE.

At the canyon – the release location – there'd be zero casualties. But as the poison flowed downstream, there would be 1,120 deaths, then 9,470, then over a million.

Wily ran back to the dune buggy and roared out of Lake Havansu City.

"Ignore the helicopter, Albert," he said into his headset. "It's a trick. Train all the cameras on to the Grand Canyon. Send the drone there, too. Tell PSSST to dispatch all their agents to the scene. That's where Klara's putting on her show."

"How can you be so sure, Wily?" Albert replied.

"She made a schoolgirl error," said Wily.

The Grand Canyon was over a hundred kilometres away, but Wily drove the dune buggy offroad, ploughing up hills and bumping over rocks, veering past cactuses and screeching through gorges.

Within the hour, he had pulled up at the Grand Canyon skywalk – a glass-bottomed viewing platform halfway along the canyon's western edge. He ran to the edge and gazed down at the river flowing lazily through the deep valley below but there was no sign of Klara.

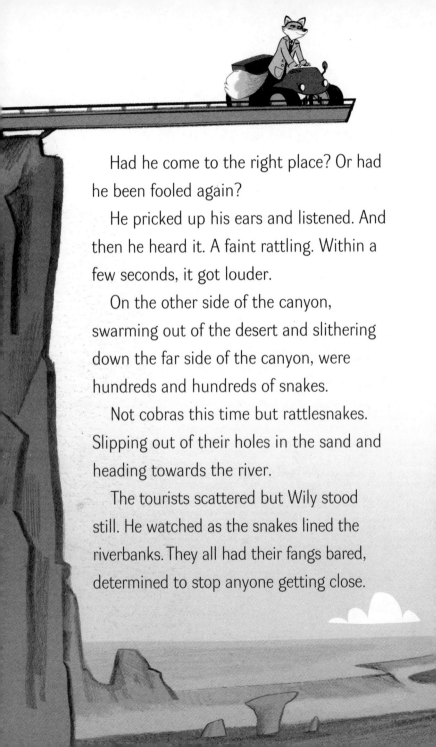

Had he come to the right place? Or had he been fooled again?

He pricked up his ears and listened. And then he heard it. A faint rattling. Within a few seconds, it got louder.

On the other side of the canyon, swarming out of the desert and slithering down the far side of the canyon, were hundreds and hundreds of snakes.

Not cobras this time but rattlesnakes. Slipping out of their holes in the sand and heading towards the river.

The tourists scattered but Wily stood still. He watched as the snakes lined the riverbanks. They all had their fangs bared, determined to stop anyone getting close.

Fox glanced at his dune buggy. It wasn't ideal but it was all he had. He jumped in and drove to the edge of the canyon. The slope was almost vertical.

On the opposite ridge, he saw another dune buggy. An animal climbed out. Klara.

"IF YOU THINK YOU CAN STOP ME," shouted Klara, "YOU'RE AS DUMB AS THAT DONKEY."

She held out the vial of poison.

"THE DONKEY'S FINE," Wily yelled back. "BECAUSE I HAVE THE ANTIDOTE."

He held up his bottle. There was only a drop of antidote left in it. But Klara didn't know that.

Klara snarled and jumped back in her buggy. Then she drove it over the edge of the canyon and straight down the steep side.

Wily put his foot down and did the same.

They were both bumping and jolting down the steep sides of the canyon, heading for the river in the middle.

Wily drove faster and faster.

Klara did the same.

Just before he reached the river, Wily hit the brakes. He flew out of the front seat and hurtled over the snakes.

Klara did the same.

They collided in mid-air, right over the river, and grabbed each other by the throats as they dropped into the water.

Underwater, they struggled. As long as she was in the river, Klara couldn't release the poison. Wily just had to keep her here until Albert's drone arrived with more antidote.

They came to the surface for air.

Keep her talking, Wily thought. "OK, Klara," he said. "How did you do it?"

"Which part?" said Klara. "The part where I cracked Menes's code in – like – half an hour? Or the part where I broke out of prison? Or the part where I found the poison while you were still pottering around the pyramids?"

The current was pushing them downstream.

"All of it," said Wily.

"I'll tell you later," said Klara. "First I have to kill you."

They plunged underwater again, wrestling and tussling.

When they surfaced, Wily heard a low whine above him. The drone!

Except it wasn't. It was Albert, riding a flying carpet.

"I managed to finish the new carpet after all!" Albert said. "So I decided to deliver the antidote in person."

Wily grinned.

Klara looked up and growled. "I've got a surprise for you, old friend."

She pulled her arm out of the water and spoke into her watch. "Snuggles! Attack!"

Wily saw a small shape zipping out of Klara's dune buggy. It zoomed through the air towards Albert.

"Remember my old toy, Captain Snuggles?" said Klara. "The one you and your friends stole at school! The one you tricked me with in Paris! Well, meet Captain Snuggles Mark Two."

Wily looked up and saw what looked like Klara's old soft toy. Except this time it was a robot puffin with rocket blasters attached to its back and pistols for wings. It was firing fireballs at Albert, who was swerving to avoid them.

"Wily!" Albert shrieked in terror.

"Now let's deal with you, my old friend," said Klara. She shoved Wily underwater just as he saw Albert's carpet being clipped by a fireball.

This time they struggled for what seemed like hours. They dived underwater, coming up for brief gulps of air before sinking back under.

Finally Klara said, "Time to let go, Wily."

Wily looked confused.

Klara held up her wrist. A rattlesnake's tail was looped around it. Another rattlesnake's tail was looped around the first rattlesnake's head. In fact, there was a long unbroken chain of snakes attaching Klara to the bank.

She let go of Wily's collar and waved. As the rattlesnakes started to pull her ashore, Wily was hurled downstream.

He was being dragged into a set of rapids towards a great waterfall. Wily could hear the powerful boom of the water crashing down. If he got swept over, the waterfall would finish him off.

He tried to swim against the current but it was pointless.

Then there was a plop beside him and Albert's head appeared next to his.

"I held out for as long as I could," Albert gasped.

"You did brilliantly, old friend," Wily gasped back. "Do you still have the antidote?"

Albert shook his head and looked ashamed. "The lid flew off in my battle with the puffin and most of it leaked out. I managed to save about a quarter."

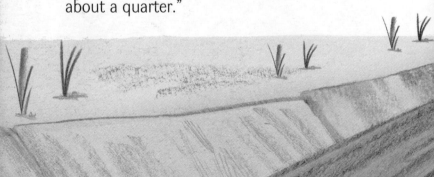

"Hmm," said Wily, inspecting the bottle that Albert was holding up. "But it's powerful stuff."

"Oh yes," said Albert. "It's super concentrated."

"Good," Wily replied. "Then we're not washed up yet."

They were about fifty metres from the waterfall. The churning was getting louder and louder.

As they were swept closer to the drop, Wily cried, "Albert, grab that rock!"

There was a boulder just behind them. Albert grabbed one side of it and Wily clung on to the other.

"It's super slippery, Wily," Albert whimpered.

"I know," Wily said, "just hang on for thirty seconds more." Wily heard a sound above them and spotted Captain Snuggles overhead, clutching the vial of poison in his beak.

Klara was on the bank, looking triumphant.

"You're losing your grip, Wily. You can watch me poison the river, while you and your antidote get washed over the waterfall!"

"OK, Klara, you win!" Wily said. "You were the best at school and you're the best now."

"Too RIGHT," cried Klara.

"I'm a goner," Wily called out. "Go on, tip the poison in. Pour it all over us. I don't care any more."

"That's rather a good idea," Klara sneered. She spoke into her watch. "Snuggles, pour the poison into the water around Wily Fox and his

mole friend so they're the FIRST to die."

Snuggles positioned himself directly above them and tipped the bottle upside down. The glowing liquid dropped through the sky.

At that second, Wily used all of his remaining strength to propel himself directly into the path of the poison. He opened his jaws wide and swallowed it. Every last drop.

"W-what?" Klara stammered.

Wily's stomach fizzed and his eyes bulged.

"An-ti-dote?" he croaked as he was sucked into the rapids. Albert leaped towards Wily and clamped the bottle of antidote to his lips, tipping the liquid down his throat.

"NO!" Klara howled. "SNAKES, ATTACK! SNUGGLES, ATTACK!"

A second later, the dam was alive with activity. PSSST helicopters roared into the sky. PSSST trucks thundered along the banks.

A giant net dropped from a helicopter on to Captain Snuggles and sent him splashing into the river. A second net covered Klara.

Meanwhile Wily and Albert were being churned around in the rapids, barely conscious.

Then Albert felt someone grab his collar.

Wily felt someone grab his arm.

"Need a lift?" said Sybil, pulling them out of the rapids. She hooked them into her harness and a PSSST helicopter began winching them to safety.

Albert and Wily smiled at her.

"Home and dry," Wily said.

Back in London, Wily was in Basil's office. Piled on the desk were Egyptian vases, Viking jewellery and more.

"Sorry, I know you wanted to analyze the poison," said Wily, "but it's all gone. Hopefully this will make up for it."

"But how? Who?" stammered Basil.

"Klara and Dimitri have been buying – and stealing – artefacts for decades. PSSST seized all of them," Wily said. "And now they belong to the British Museum."

Basil picked up one of the bracelets. "This is the Cairo Crystal. It went missing from Egypt centuries ago." He pointed to a silver sword. "And this is Zeus's spear," he added. "We were never sure if it really existed."

"Better than a vial of poison, eh?"

"You really do solve crime in record time, Mr Fox," said Basil. "How can the museum ever repay you?"

"There's no need," said Wily with a smile.

"We could have a room devoted to you!" Basil exclaimed. "The Wily Fox Wing!"

Wily shook his head. "I'd rather not make an exhibition of myself," he said, "and besides…" He winked. "I'm not history yet."